Giverny

Susan C. Barto

THIRD EDITION

Library of Congress Control Number:

99-74450

ISBN-10: 0-9712516-4-9

ISBN-13: 9780971251649

Gary Drury's Publishing™

Kentucky

Produced in The United States of America.

DEDICATION

MY BELOVED HUSBAND,
and MY SON BILL.

CONTENTS

Giverny

Until they took a bus to Giverny, Sally felt that their third trip to Paris had been a flop—the vacation from hell. While they were waiting for their luggage at Charles de Gaulle, a shot rang out. They missed seeing the bullet's whizzing by or hitting any mark, but Sally gasped in astonishment as a man ran for his life while two gendarmes chased him across the airport past her and Richard.

"My Lord," Sally said. "What an experience. Do you think they'll catch him?"

"I don't know," Richard said. "But we don't know enough French to follow it in the papers."

After the excitement in the airport, the drive to the hotel seemed tame and boring. Seated in the van provided by the airline, they watched as the first few passengers exited at the luxury hotels and the next few passengers exited at the medium luxury hotels until they and one lone passenger remained in the van. Sally began to feel an unpleasant thrill of fear as to what kind of accommodations waited for them as she knew that each stop at a hotel seemed to be a step down from the previous stop. This vacation, the airline had chosen the hotel for them.

Fortunately, the van made only one more stop for the three of them in the Bastille district which looked dirty for Paris to Sally. She thought of Paris as whisk broom clean. Apparently, the Bastille section was an exception. The hotel looked quaint from the outside and lobby, and as they had to wait until their room was made up, the amiable hotel clerk presented Sally and Richard with large cups of foaming café au lait. An auspicious beginning. As they accepted the steaming café au lait Richard inquired as to whether the hotel clerk had heard about the shot fired at the airport.

"Oui," he replied. "The gendarmes chased a terrorist all through Charles de Gaulle, but he managed to elude them somehow. He'd been caught with a homemade bomb. Naturally, the police are still chasing him."

Sally felt struck with horror when she saw the appalling room that appeared when the bell boy opened the door. Her first impression of the room stuck as she realized that the room was not only tiny but dingy as well. After entering, she saw that the bathroom was at least clean with spotless towels, but the bed which to the hotel's credit had clean white pressed sheets had a board sitting under the thin mattress instead of a box spring. As if this weren't bad enough, the bed was so low to the floor that Sally wondered if she could get up from bed gracefully. The room, however, overlooked a picturesque courtyard with a full view of an apartment house where young couples and their small offspring were visible. Finally, Sally and Richard observed that the room had a small kitchenette where a neat green box covered a minuscule stove. Obviously, the hotel doubled as a temporary apartment house.

Richard, seeming to tread gently around this situation said, "Sal, do you want me to ask the manager for another room? We couldn't possibly get another hotel at this short notice."

"What I intend to do is scream loudly," Sally said close to tears, "and then I guess we'll just have to accept this room. After all, we're in Paris. Let's just spend all our time out of this room." And then she let loose with the promised scream.

Since it was by then lunch time they proceeded to explore the area around the Bastille district and stopped at a corner café for jambon aux baguettes and cups of the foaming, marvelous café au lait. However, their vacation contained problems no matter how bright a face they painted on it. There was only one fine restaurant in the whole district, and when they attempted to find the first class restaurant where they had eaten many meals their last trip to Paris they lucked out in making reservations only with the help of the accommodating hotel clerk behind the desk who also tried to get them a taxi with no luck since the rush and dinner hours were the busiest in Paris. Sally said,

"Let's walk to a taxi stand. Something has to come along eventually." She then turned to the clerk and asked again whether he had heard about the shot fired at the airport as he was listening to the radio.

"Non, Madame, but they will catch him I am sure."

"I just hope he isn't planning another homemade bomb for our return flight," Sally said only half joking.

They finally found a cab, but by then it was so late they feared their reservation at Aux Trois Portes might have expired. Following the superb dinner, the maitre d'hailed them a cab, but after this experience they didn't venture out of the Bastille district at the dinner hour again for fear of being stranded in a district too far away for a feasible walk. After that first night's elegant dinner they contented themselves with dinners at the local good restaurants where no English was spoken. Armed with only Sally's high school French they struggled valiantly each night to order something that they would recognize when it arrived.

The first two days they did the Musee d'Orsay and the Louvre, but it was the third day of their vacation that Sally came alive. A trip to Giverny, planned by the airline occurred smack in the center of the week. They hailed a cab and arrived at the bus terminal around lunch time with about an hour and a half to spare.

"Do you want to go to the Louvre across the street and have lunch?" Richard asked for they had lunched in the good restaurant at the Louvre the other day and enjoyed themselves.

"No, Richard, look how far the line in front of the ticket booth to get into the museum is."

"Look, right here next to where we meet the bus is a hotel with a restaurant that overlooks the street and the tourists. Do you want lunch here?"

"Why not? But it looks frightfully expensive."

"This is our vacation, remember."

Sitting in the well appointed dining room at a window seat. Sally felt as if her real vacation started now. The food and service in the hotel had the finesse Sally had expected from the hotel the airline had booked for them. This would be the last time she'd ever allow the airline to choose. She'd had trepidations about that in the beginning, but Richard had felt that the airline would never steer you wrong as they wanted your repeat business. They lingered over lunch. They found their bus easily, and Sally wanted to sit on the first floor while all the other passengers clamored for the second floor of the double decker bus. Only Sally and Richard and the guide remained in the bottom of the bus to Sally's delight. As they meandered through the districts of Paris, a bonus of this particular bus trip, the guide reeled off the by now familiar sights of the city—the Eiffel Tower, the Arc de Triomphe, the Champs-Elysees as well as the Louvre and the Musee d'Orsay (one on either side of the Seine) where they had previously visited this trip. As soon as they were out of the city and headed in the direction of Giverny in the country-side, the guide commenced talking about Monet and in particular his love affair with Giverny.

The guide informed them that Monet came to Giverny about 40 miles northwest of Paris in 1883. Giverny was given to him late in life by the French government. Here Monet created an ideal world for both personal and artistic reasons. Although he traveled regularly as far as London and Venice, it was this landscape within a two-mile radius of Giverny that he painted most frequently for the rest of his life. With his famous Haystacks pictures, begun in 1890, Monet began painting in series, often painting several canvases at once so as to capture the scene in changing light and various weather conditions.

Water lilies totally occupied Monet towards the end of his career. Monet did extensive gardening and had a pond dug out and planted with water lilies in 1893. He adopted the water lily motif for his paintings in the summer of 1889. in a large-scale series he worked for twenty years or more trying to capture every nuance of the flowers and water. The subjects Monet painted at Giverny reflect his imagination as well as reality. His final paintings of the water lilies boarder on abstraction.

Once off the bus and actually in the gardens of Giverny, Sally felt overwhelmed by scent. It was as though some magician had uncorked a thousand perfume bottles at once and released the myriad fragrances. The visual beauty assaulted her senses as well as she observed tulips and bunches of blooms she couldn't recognize but whose beauty caressed her eyes. Here Richard snapped pictures of the gardens and Sally in swift profusion. The house was all in yellow and blue inside, and many of Monet's paintings resided there. The kitchen carried on the yellow and blue theme with tiles, and the house shone. They capped off their tour of Giverny by visiting the bridge and the water lily pond. Sally thrilled to the pleasure of seeing the scene where Monet had painted all those glorious water lilies. Exhausted with pleasure, they went to a little café in the rear and shared a coke after stopping in the gift shop where Sally purchased a barrette painted with a scene of the flowers in the garden here at Giverny.

When they reembarked on the bus to go back to Paris, they discovered that for the return trip they were not alone on the first level. A chatty couple sat in the seats across the aisle from them.

"Did you hear?" asked the man. "The Paris police caught that airport terrorist."

As if the heavenly trip didn't suffice, Sally delighted at this news. Giverny constituted a fresh start to their Paris trip as it had been a fresh start for Monet's painting.

Bonnie And David

David belonged to the Senior class while Bonnie took her place among the lowly Sophomores. For a Sophomore, dating a Senior gave a girl a certain cachet. Her prestige zoomed up a few notches while she dated him. Bonnie rode high on a cloud while she dated David, and she never understood exactly how it happened. David and Bonnie formed half of a chemistry foursome. The chemistry class divided itself into groups of four with each group sitting and working at the same table. David and Bonnie mixed formulas together, and their personal chemistry exploded at about the same time their first experiment did. David's crowd in the Senior class comprised the top crowd, so Bonnie too was in the top crowd while she dated David. His friends called him the Boston Bean as he was a find from Massachusetts.

Bonnie began to comprehend that she might be floundering in waters over her head on her first date with David. He picked her up in his own car, another plus, and took her to the finest movie theater three towns away. Her nervousness during the movie impeded her understanding of it as she worried about how the second half of the evening would go. After the movie David commenced necking with Bonnie before he even moved the car out of the parking lot. After trying more moves than Bonnie allowed him to complete, David finally left the parking lot and drove to a drive-in for hamburgers and shakes. This comprised the beginning of their dating life which began in May and continued for its first cycle until the end of the summer.

David worked part-time at the post office, and Bonnie formed the habit of dropping by there on her way home from cokes in town with her friends. The men who worked in the post office knew that she dated David, and they kidded her when she arrived to mail her letters. Each evening David's white car appeared in front of Bonnie's house, and they attended all the movies and parties of the summer together. David's friends all had cars, and often a crowd of his friends would show up at her house looking for David, which infuriated Bonnie's Dad.

The fourth of July seemed glorious as David's family threw a barbecue during the day and David invited Bonnie, who proceeded to meet his family and visiting cousins. That evening Bonnie and David and his Senior crowd went to Memorial Field and watched the fireworks which seemed particularly glorious as Bonnie sat in the dark on a blanket holding David's hand and watching the skyrockets explode releasing a display of brilliant arrays of color across the sky. Also that summer Bonnie and David rode to the shore with a friend of David's who drove a red convertible and his steady. They spent many sunny and sometimes even cloudy afternoons on the beach. The beach often caused David to wax eloquent compliments to Bonnie saying,

"You look so natural on the beach without your make-up. Your beauty is like that of the rocks, the sand and the surf."

The struggle after the dates concluded continued all summer until it escalated into a break-up with David's asserting,

"If you were more mature, you would find sex beautiful, instead of fighting it every step of the way."

Bonnie stuck to her code of ethics even though this caused David to drop her temporarily for a waitress he met at the local diner. Bonnie presumed that this waitress must have been more mature.

Autumn came and with it came the beginning of Bonnie's junior year in high school and the start of David's Freshman year at college. Bonnie suffered each time she thought of David, but she got on with her life. Around Halloween Bonnie's Tri-Ep Hi-Y group gave a dance for which the Tri-Ep girls invited dates. Bonnie revved up her nerve and asked David. To her wonderment he accepted. When he picked her up that night he said,

"Today's my nineteenth birthday, and I'd rather spend it with you than with anyone."

Prior to the dance Bonnie had asked her girlfriend Maryann who happened to be dating a fraternity brother of David's to watch out for her as it might prove to be a difficult evening. Maryann's date, Peter, belonged to the fraternity which had just pledged David as a member. Peter replied to Maryann's request that they look after Bonnie,

"She doesn't look as though she needs any help."

From Halloween to Christmas vacation Bonnie's world twirled along in high gear. David now told Bonnie that he loved her, and she allowed him a tiny bit more leeway in the necking department. However, it was the necking problem which caused their second breakup towards the end of Christmas week and left Bonnie dateless on New Year's Eve. Maryann and Pete talked her into attending a fraternity party with them and a friend of Peter's named Harry. Bonnie decided to attend rather than wallow in her misery only because Maryann taunted her saying that this fraternity brother, Harry, wouldn't find Bonnie his type. Naturally, Bonnie turned on her charm on New Year's Eve to assure Maryann that he would so like her. He did like her, but to her surprise she liked him too. He possessed a sweetness and an intelligence coupled with a mature out-look on life that David woefully lacked. Bonnie couldn't believe that the thought this is the man I am going to marry flew into her head that night, and she kept it a secret almost even from herself.

From New Year's Eve on Bonnie and Harry began dating, and Bonnie never thought about David until the following summer when Harry went away to National Guard Camp and Bonnie ran into David in town. When he asked her to go to the movies with him that evening she accepted just to be sure that her feelings for Harry hadn't been caused by her being on the rebound from David. No sooner had David picked Bonnie up when he said,

"We could be this close again,"and he demonstrated by holding up his middle two fingers pressed together.

Bonnie fielded this with a light touch saying,

"You broke my heart twice. Do you want to go for a third time?"

David, however, didn't take no for an answer, and the unfortunate evening ended bitterly. The rancor continued as David, Harry and Pete were all in the same fraternity, and Bonnie and Harry were always running smack into David at fraternity parties and events. Once David stabbed at Bonnie when after seeing her and Harry leaving a parked car at a dance he yelled,

"I thought you didn't do things like that."

David's jabs only enforced Bonnie's feelings about how much she loved Harry, and she felt fortunate to have met him in time. Her experience with David gave her wisdom she might have acquired at a higher cost. David was popular, and women followed him around like puppy dogs. However, he used people sucking the juice out of them like he would an orange, and then tossing them away like the orange peels. Bonnie lucked out by leaving him in time. She followed his escapades during Harry's college years, and watched as he became engaged and broke it off after the wedding invitations had been mailed. Even after she and Harry happily married, David continued his tricks with women. New Year's Eve started Bonnie's move away from David and toward a mature relationship with someone who felt about her the way she felt about him giving their life and love a chance to grow and bloom.

Two French Maids

Reflecting on her friendship with Mary Jo, Sally wandered the labyrinth of all possible routes her memory could take. Thoughts of Mary Jo were triggered by a comment made by the newest Councilman's wife whom Sally met at a Council social event where she was herself a councilman's wife.

"I know you," Leonora the novice council wife said. "You were Mary Jo's best friend when we were children. I was her sister Marcie's closest friend, and I spotted you frequently with Mary Jo when I was closeted with Marcie in her room. I encountered you and Mary Jo on our mutual forays to the kitchen for cokes."

While Sally racked her brain for any remembrance of Leonora all those years ago, memories of Mary Jo flooded her mind. What a pleasant interlude in her life that had been. Sally moved into town in the third grade, and being a friendly soul managed to join the most popular and noticeable crowd at the grade school. She admired and enjoyed all the girls, but after a short time of getting to know the crowd, she and Mary Jo became close friends or in the jargon of her peers "best friends". Sally felt honored by Mary Jo's attention since Mary Jo was not only beautiful sporting a creamy complexion highlighted by rosy cheeks, but she had a shy sweet manner that didn't quite mask an infectious sense of humor. The girls were allies at school joining the activities of the group but managing to save time for private meetings of the mind and engaging in gossip and comments regarding the other girls in the class. Not to forget the girls' notice of and interest in the most popular boys in the class.

Fifth and sixth grades were a schizophrenic time in the girls' life. While each still held an interest in dolls, paper dolls, tag, and hide and seek, at the same time they scorned their own interest in these things in favor of a burgeoning curiosity about the boys in their school and the activities favored by Mary Jo's older sister, Marcie, and her crowd. Sally, too, had an older cousin who had passed from the childhood arena to become a mysterious teen. Mary Jo informed Sally when the activities they were engaging in to while away a summer afternoon would be scorned by Marcie and her friends.

In the summertime Sally and Mary Jo's friendship had time enough to ripen. They spent their mornings with a whole group of children at the park attempting to make lanyards and coasting on the swings, hanging on the monkey bars, and having marathon attempts on the teeter-totter. After lunch, however, energies flagged, and activities became more leisurely and sometimes thoughtful and intellectual. At Mary Jo's house the girls engaged in hours of board games - Monopoly, Go To The Head of The Class, Sorry, etc. Over these languid games the girls discussed life from their vantage points and the mores of the time they were living in as accepted members of their group.

Sally and Mary Jo hatched many of their more brilliant ideas on these lazy summer afternoons lolling on Mary Jo's backyard lawn such as the French maid Halloween caper, and the famous sixth grade wedding, as well as the initial plans for the club the two girls founded. As her memories were opening in front of her like the yellowing leaves of an old scrapbook, Sally realized that many of her and Mary Jo's adventures were plotted in Mary Jo's backyard as they took turns lying on the hammock and looking at the cloud formations.

Into the near paradise of Sally and Mary Jo's friendship intruded a new element in the presence of one Louise Diamond Dumont Vanderlynn. Louise moved to town sometime during the fifth grade year and introduced herself to the girls by showing off her pedigree and her unique name. She obviously had been named using family and maiden names. The girls were amused as middle names heretofore were ordinary or yucky like Abigail not strange sounding rich last names. Louise brought the ways of another place and region with her, and she was more advanced about boys than Sally and Mary Jo. Louise initiated boy hunts where the girls would meander around the town winding up at the streets where the more handsome boys lived. At this stage of their lives contact with boys occurred at school or at school related activities like the school newspaper on which both Sally and Mary Jo worked.

Once a meeting of the newspaper staff met at Sally's house, an occasion which warranted her writing about looking forward to seeing Tony and Dick at her house in her diary. That night while the young people were gathering in the living room of Sally's house, Sally's younger brother, Steve, brought Tony and Dick up to Sally's room and showed them the choicest parts of her diary, which apparently he had already read. He showed them the embarrassing entry already mentioned along with an entry mentioning the purchase of Sally's first bra. The boys roared and lustily enjoyed this foray into Sally's diary, and afterward tried to bribe Steve for more peeks at the diary. One boy offered to gift Steve with a snake if he got Sally to date him, but this happened a little bit in the future.

Gradually Louise slid into Sally and Mary Jo's circle, and she was embraced by the popular girls for all the group activities and parties, and sometimes Louise entered the rarified air of Mary Jo and Sally's company enlarging their twosome into a threesome. The three went to girl scout camp and enjoyed two weeks of togetherness, fresh air, sleeping in tents, swimming, boating and hiking. They shared the same tent and continued their rather exclusive friendship. Sometime, however, at the beginning of the sixth grade, Louise moved away again, and Sally and Mary Jo's friendship continued without a tear in the seam.

As sixth grade Halloween costumes Sally and Mary Jo wore French maid costumes sewn by Sally's grandmother and consisting of short black uniforms with a ruffled cap and white frilled apron. Both girls made a splash at school and later when their entire group embarked on their marathon trick and treating Mary Jo and Sally got many admiring comments on their unusual costumes. This had been one of Mary Jo's bolt of lightening ideas on one lazy summer afternoon in her backyard. Sally usually went right along and embroidered and festooned Mary Jo's ideas with plans of her own.

The culmination of sixth grade activities and the peak of the events involving their crowd was a mock wedding of two of the young people who were at the time precociously going steady. This plan too Mary Jo hatched in her backyard with Sally's egging her on. Soon the entire sixth grade was caught up in the wedding plans. A best man, maid of honor and bridesmaids waited for the big day. Sally's mother fell under the pressure and agreed to host the event, and the class managed to shock and intrigue their male sixth grade teacher, Mr. Fenn, who was more often than not surprised by the rather too advanced for their age group activities of this class. The mock wedding was held and carried out without a quiver of trouble except for someone's putting a coke bottle on the grand piano during the ceremony. Sally's horrified mother managed to snatch the offending bottle off the mahogany piano before the dreaded white ring could appear.

During this period a coed movie party occurred on a Saturday afternoon, and a group of sixth grade girls attended a Robin Hood movie with a group of boys who had previously asked them to accompany them. Mary Jo and Sally and the members of a club they formed that year were included in this much planned and talked about event. That Spring Sally threw a party for her group inviting both boys and girls, and the party was a booming success ending up with a memorable game of Spin the Bottle played with the theme from Moulin Rouge on the record player in the background. The Spin the Bottle game was the first for the entire class, and sadly it helped to move the young people farther away from childhood than they had been before. The party was held just before sixth grade graduation, and the following fall Sally's life changed with an unpleasant crash. Junior High started turning Sally's life upside down.

Sally was shocked by the unpleasant turn of events unfolding about her because her dreams of Junior High were so different from the harsh reality. Mary Jo's house was across the street from the Junior High, and Sally envisioned many afternoons after school dreaming and planning with Mary Jo as she had before. The habit of several years of a close friendship was hard to break, and indeed Sally had never even thought of it. Mary Jo was sick with the flu the first two dramatic weeks of Junior High. Here at the new school Sally's popular grade school group was scattered with the girls' being placed into different home rooms and intermingled with the kids from the other grade schools in town. Sally, a sociable person, found this an unexpected opportunity to meet new people with perhaps different backgrounds and tales to tell. Only one boy and one girl from her former crowd were in her home room, and she therefore began to bond with the new people dropping in every day on Mary Jo to check in and see about the state of her health and fill her in about Junior High. One unforgettable and agonizing afternoon Mary Jo commented to Sally,

"I see you're not in with the popular crowd anymore."

Sally, too stunned to react, just looked at Mary Jo not quite understanding what she meant. Mary Jo went on to say,

"Apparently, our old crowd has regrouped and has added a few of the most desirable new girls."

Sally thought about this and belatedly realized that she had seen some members of her old group and other girls standing at one particular entrance of the school and using one certain sweet shop in town after school, but she hadn't given it much thought feeling it natural that groups might regroup, and the girls would embrace girls from other schools as she had done, but she always knew that she and Mary Jo would continue. What did the forming of groups have to do with them?

Looking back Sally could see clearly things she had not been aware of then. Her high school was a snobbish one. While in grade school, all types of people could be incorporated into a crowd for their unique qualities. Once Junior High started the group was sifted much more finely, and most didn't make it. Sally was intuitive enough to sense that this was a sea change in her friendship with Mary Jo. Mary Jo's being influenced by the old crowd was considering Sally not only on her own merits, but on the merits of the other people Sally spent time with. Maybe the new friends Sally fraternized with and the friend from her old grade school, Jean, didn't measure up to the new Junior High standards. Sally had begun walking home with Jean.

Losing Mary Jo as a best friend sobered Sally and hastened her on the more grown up road of Junior High. Always she and Mary Jo would have a special connection and feeling for each other, and once in eighth grade when Sally was dating a boy in the top crowd she and Mary Jo found themselves briefly in the same group again. Sally savored this time, and she was pleased that throughout high school and on the few occasions when they came across each other after marriage and babies had further changed them that there was still a spark. But the best friend intimacy had been shattered that afternoon when a kind of innate snobbery that Sally never knew Mary Jo possessed came to the fore and exploded the paradise of her childhood like the snake in the garden.

As she stood there at the cocktail party memories surrounding her, Sally was relieved to realize that almost all of them were happy.

The Littlest Elf

Tiddly-Winks lived at the North Pole. During the thick of the Christmas season, Tiddly-Winks and the other elves felt swamped with work. This avalanche of toy making did not bother Tiddly-Winks especially. He suffered even when many weeks remained till Christmas, and the work load lightened. Tiddly-Winks felt sad because he was the littlest elf, not the youngest elf by far, since Tiddly-Winks at sixteen had been making toys for quite a while, but definitely the smallest. No, Tiddly-Winks stayed blue because he measured too few feet to comfortably reach the high, long worktable where all the elves worked on the toys in a friendly, communal fashion, and his hands were too miniature to handle the tools proficiently. Therefore, Santa judged his finished toys as poor.

Santa provided a huge stack of his own phone books for Tiddly-Winks to sit on so he could reach the worktable (Santa's phone books looked unique because the listings consisted of only children's names and phone numbers even though Santa never had time to telephone any of the children as far as Tiddly-Winks could tell.) This particular December afternoon the littlest elf felt even sadder than usual. Santa had refused a finished toy of his that he, Tiddly-Winks, thought the best he had ever completed. Since Santa rejected all of his toys, Tiddly-Winks should have been used to it, but no one ever grew to like censure or rejection, and he hated the laughter of the other elves every time Santa turned down another one of his works of art.

Actually, Santa seemed to mind these failures as much as Tiddly-Winks did. Tiddly-Winks knew that Santa felt sorry for him, but Santa couldn't allow an inferior toy to pass and risk disappointing a child. Tiddly-Winks noticed that Santa seemed to be always thinking of what he could do to make life more bearable for Tiddly-Winks. He observed that Mrs. Santa, too, tried to make him happy by always putting an extra marshmallow in his cocoa or extra sprinkles on his Christmas butter cookies, but nothing helped Tiddly-Winks as he knew he was a flop.

On this day just a week before Christmas, Tiddly-Winks started on another toy knowing as he did so that Santa would reject this one too. As he was painting a wagon red, Tiddly-Winks felt struck as though by a light-ening bolt with an idea. He ran out of the workshop all the way to Santa's house. He burst in on Mrs. Santa and Santa just as they were drinking hot chocolate. Tiddly-Winks approached Santa and whispered in his ear, while Mrs. Santa smiled kindly at him. After Tiddly-Winks was sure Santa heard his suggestion, he went back to the workshop.

Later that day in the midst of the turmoil at the work-bench, Santa came back into the workshop carrying a brand spanking new high stool.

"Tiddly-Winks," said Santa. "I made this high stool especially for you. I have decided to follow your advice and make you our quality control elf to save me the labor of checking out the toys for the children. You above all elves know what a good toy is since you have made all the possible mistakes and know what they are. I trust you to check out all the toys scrupulously before putting on your elfin seal of approval. Come here my littlest elf."

Tiddly-Winks could hardly speak for the joy coursing through him. From that moment his life changed. Now he liked his job on all days of the year. He became a super quality control elf.

Going Steady

Their friendship blossomed in the cafeteria where his crowd of boys merged with her crowd of girls, The two compatible groups shared a lunch table, and dated when school let out. Don at first seemed to Liz to be a pal and a confidant. He'd just broken up bitterly with one of Liz's friends, and she offered him comfort and solace. She, too, had recently split with an on again off again boyfriend, and enjoyed this shared commiseration. Things progressed rapidly from here, and soon Liz and Don started walking home together-a convenient arrangement since they lived close to each other, only two blocks separated their houses. Spring that year bloomed with an incredible softness, and the mild fragrant air spurred their budding romance on. That Spring Don belonged to the high school's track team. He specialized in running and sprinting. Liz began attending the track meets, at least when they took place at home.

One Friday afternoon about an hour before the 3 p.m. bell rang Don rushed panting up to Liz's corridor committee post. She stood in the hall before and after each bell trying to prevent running in the halls, etc. and she got to come to classes late and leave early.

"Liz, I have a track meet in an hour. Hold my ring for me for luck, and let me carry your silver and turquoise Indian arrowhead necklace. I have a feeling this will bring me a win."

Liz thrilled to this proposal. It felt so close to being asked to go steady, She accepted his ring and spent the next hour explaining how even though she held Don's ring they didn't have a going, steady pact. She felt proud at the track meet, and Don did indeed win his races. This started a Spring track meet tradition. Each track meet, whether at home or away, Don retrieved her arrowhead and gave her his ring for safekeeping, and he had an extraordinarily successful season.

A few weeks before school ended for the summer break, Nancy hosted an end of school party to which Liz had been invited and instructed to bring along a date. She promptly asked Don who accepted looking, mysterious and smiling an enigmatic smile. Liz wondered what was up, and half feared that tonight he would ask her to go steady officially. Why this long hoped for circumstance should make her feel frightened and have a brief flash of dread she didn't comprehend. Sure enough, as soon as the party ended, Don walked Liz to the brook by the Memorial Field field house, and looking down into the water asked Liz to go steady. Liz, who heretofore, had been praying for this moment said,

"I'd be honored to wear your ring, Thank you for asking."

The fun part of this happening was buying a chain for the ring, as the fashion at that time was to wear a boy's ring on a chain around your neck, and watching her friends' faces express surprise when they glimpsed the ring. Also fun, Liz thought, was observing her father's not too pleased reaction, although he gave his begrudging permission. Liz's status shot up with the new going steady appellation. The best part seemed to Liz to be not worrying whether or not you would have a date for the important end of school parties and events. She and Don spent a good deal of time together.

The summer spun on with trips to the New Jersey shore at the fore. Don and his friends enlisted the driving skills of their older friends, and a whole group would head for the beach together. Once ensconced on a blanket on the sand the couples necked , the warm sun and hot sand spurring them on. Only the laws of decency and indecent exposure prevented the boys from trying to go too far-after all they were on display. The girl's figures were on display in the merciless rays of the sun. Liz's figure more than passed muster in every respect except for her Birra thighs — her mother's side of the family had chubby thighs. Don bemoaned this one flaw in her otherwise pleasing appearance, and nagged her about losing weight in just her thighs since he loved the rest of her anatomy. Since Liz knew this to be impossible she ignored this less than attractive behavior on Don's part. Her ego felt salved since Don's friends gave her more than appreciative glances in her swim suit and even bothered to tell Don how sexy she looked, Don's personality left much to be desired as he rarely treated his friends with the kindness and respect Liz felt he ought to show them.

Don's family vacationed in Nantucket each August, and as their separation drew near and soon loomed over their heads the couple began to treat each other more tenderly as though they realized that they held something so fragile it threatened to break apart. While Don was in Nantucket Liz's plans included two weeks of babysitting along, with a good friend at the shore in a fashionable community. This job constituted a plum, and she and Jean looked forward to it all summer. She and Jean enjoyed the two weeks of sun and surf. Their duties seemed relatively minor and certainly not irksome. They had one free day a week and spent it on the boardwalk laughing and having such fun that an elderly man spotted them wending their way home after their day out and looking so happy that he mourned his lost youth out loud to them. Don and Liz exchanged letters, although Don's letters frequently annoyed Liz as they mentioned girls he had met in Nantucket, two of whom - twins - would be attending their high school this coming fall. She retaliated by alluding to her own romantic encounters although they occurred rarely as she honored their going, steady even though it appeared as though he had relaxed the edict.

Happily for Liz the summer burned itself out and with the crisp fall air came the first day of school and her reunion with Don. At first they felt passionate with each other due to the month long separation. They had geometry together, and this seemed a true bonus. However, after the novelty of their reunion wore off, Don reverted to his old ways including his wandering eye and his assumption that because Liz came endowed with big beautiful breasts she also came equipped with a desire to make out as much as he cared to. This misinformation on Don's part caused frequent bitter arguments between the two causing Liz to constantly return Don's ring to him right in the middle of geometry class much to the amusement of the other kids. The ring constituted a sore point with Liz as she had inadvertently been the cause of the ring's having been stolen the one time she wore it on her finger and took it off to wash her hands. As soon as she'd left the ladies' room she remembered the ring and rushed back for it only to find it gone. Liz used all her babysitting money to buy Don a new gold signet ring, and instead of thanking her he remained critical about the ring's initial loss.

Liz felt that Don's final injury to her dignity occurred after she met his older brother. Don seemed to be thrilled with Larry's appraisal of Liz. Don said, "Larry told me that you look as though you'd be good in bed."

"This you consider to be a compliment?"

"From one brother to another, yes."

After this insult their going steady limped along finally reaching its climax at the annual Hi Y hayride given by Don's Hi Y group. After an initial fun start, the hay ride degenerated into a wrestling match with Liz's grabbing at Don's hands, and Don's continuing to grope and exclaiming,

"It's the lurching of the wagon causing me to touch you where I wouldn't."

This time when Liz gave back his ring Don didn't protest and immediately return it. Liz never wanted to go steady again. She'd had it with this nonsense, and each time a boy asked her she demurred. However, a few years later when she fell in love for real when the young man she loved proposed she felt no stab of dread and no sense of unhappiness . The going steady adventure remained behind her a part of her nostalgic past.

Seeing The Sphinx

Sarah Jane had dreamed all her life of going to Paris, and Robert's being an amateur Egyptologist desired to go to Egypt with equal fervor. Accordingly, the two planned a combined trip taking Egypt Air to Paris, staying for a week, and then flying to Egypt, staying for another week, and flying home from Egypt. The thought of seeing Egypt filled Sarah Jane with fear although she didn't know whether it was the heat, not knowing what to wear, or a combination of' the two. However, she felt so thrilled about the Paris trip that she acquiesced rapidly. The week in Paris passed by for Sarah Jane In a blissful blur, and before she knew It they were winging their way to Egypt on what turned out to be an extremely bumpy flight.

They hooked up with their touring car at the airport, and headed for their luxury hotel in the soft Egyptian night air indigenous to Egypt in early May. Sarah Jane thought that the foliage looked like a combination of Florida's trees and plants and a luxurious jungle. The heat surrounding them was mild in the evening rather than fierce or hot. She asked the guide,

"How hot can we expect it to be during the heat of the afternoon?"

"In Cairo right now in the high seventies."

Sarah Jane felt relieved. This she could handle. The ride seemed pleasant, and the guide informed them of other trips they could take outside of Cairo. Since an airplane ride to Luxor and Karnak cost more than they had planned to spend, Sarah Jane offered,

"Robert, why don't you plan to fly to those cities, and leave me here in Cairo? It's only for a day isn't it? You'd be home by evening?"

The guide concurred, and Robert agreed to Sarah Jane's plan, and a midweek trip to Luxor and Karnak became part of their itinerary. As they entered Cairo Sarah Jane's excitement reached a fever pitch, and didn't diminish when she caught sight of their five star hotel. In Paris she'd contented herself with a small well-appointed hotel, but in the wilds of Egypt, she'd insisted on five star. The hotel looked gorgeous, and their room came equipped with living room complete with a circular brass table and a television that featured continuous American movies in English. After ascertaining that room service was available for breakfast the next morning, they drifted off to sleep feeling content.

The first day they wanted to get their bearings around Cairo and inquire about touring cars to take them to the pyramids the following day. Their first adventure consisted of taking a touring car to the bazaar. What a cacophonous racket blasted their ear drums when they exited the car and what a feast for their eyes. Sarah Jane collected cats and wanted to purchase an Egyptian cat on a pedestal wearing earrings if possible. Passing many small stalls and shops and failing in love with a sleeping, purring cat in front of one of the shops, Sarah Jane crooned "Nefer" which means beautiful to the feline causing what must have been the cat's owner to peer suspiciously out of the door of his shop. With no further incident they found themselves in front of a shop which featured the very cat Sarah Jane desired. She knew enough to try to bargain, but she realized how feeble her bargaining skills were when not only did her first offer meet with their delighted approval, but they received a gift which the shopkeeper called a cachet consisting of two colorful sand filled bottles. The only unpleasant incident occurred as they reached the meeting place to get back into their touring car, and a young boy accosted them asking for baksheesh (money or a tip). Because of the great number of children begging for alms, Sarah Jane and Robert felt obliged to refuse. The child whose mouth was covered with crumbs commenced spitting at their cab when their driver said something to the child in Egyptian, and the incident ended.

The driver expressed an interest in being their driver on any day trips they might plan. Accordingly, Robert engaged his services arranging for him to meet them in front of their hotel early the following morning. After a nice lunch at the hotel following the bazaar, they walked a couple of blocks to the Cairo Museum, and Robert found himself in heaven, and even Sarah Jane thrilled to the ancient statutes and especially to the treasures that abounded in the Tutankhamen collection. The gold alone took her breath away. After visiting the Cairo Museum they traversed the area around and across the street from their hotel and discovered a fine French hairdressers in the hotel Sarah Jane planned to visit and a marvelous shopping center across the street containing a bookstore featuring books printed in English and a magnificent store which carried Egyptian caftans.

The next morning started their adventures. Promptly at 8:30 a.m. the driver appeared to drive them to the pyramids. Their first stop was at Giza which housed the most famous pyramids and also the Sphinx. Robert quickly advanced near the pyramid and headed for the inside tour. Sarah Jane felt that the close enclosed space might be too claustrophobic, and consequently she demurred. However, she met up with a man with a camel who asked her whether she'd like either a ride on the beast or her picture taken with him. She turned down the ride, but acquiesced as to the picture, and he handed her a turban to put on and a staff to hold. Equipped with these props, Sarah Jane felt in the spirit of the adventure. The camel driver proceeded to take almost an entire role of film which worried Sarah Jane as she knew Robert had plans for the rest of that role of film. Fortunately, Robert carried extra roles in his pockets. At one point during the photo shoot, Sarah Jane became convinced that the camel was going to spit, and she expressed her fears to the driver who responded,

"Lady, I know my camel, and he's not about to spit."

After Robert emerged from the pyramid, he, Sarah Jane and the guide wended their way to the Sphinx. Gazing at that mysterious wonder of the world, Sarah Jane knew why it was considered to be enigmatic, and why Napoleon felt so spooked after seeing the pyramids and the Sphinx. The guide told her that legend had it that luck would come to a honeymoon couple who spent the night sleeping near the Pyramids. They felt that the legend seemed interesting, but made them glad not be honeymooners anymore. From the site of the pyramids, the guide took them to a place which made papyrus, and they bought a piece, and then he guided them to a place which featured gold cartouches. After a stimulating round of bargaining, Robert purchased an eighteen caret gold cartouche for Sarah Jane and also a sterling silver one. For himself, he purchased a key chain with a sterling silver cartouche. The driver then took them to an elegant authentically Egyptian place for lunch pointing out a spot on the Nile where he claimed Moses had been found in his basket. Sarah Jane smiled and looked at Robert who could scarcely hide his skepticism.

That afternoon after lunch the driver took them to see the Step Pyramid. This Pyramid is even older than the Giza Pyramid. The design seemed more primitive, and they walked all around it. Standing and seeing the Step Pyramid at a distance Sarah Jane felt that she was about as big as a speck of dust on God's eyelash. At the Step Pyramid lived a large pack of wild dogs who seemed quite tame, and in fact existed on dry dog food the people brought with them to feed the dogs. Stray cats too lived all over Egypt and broke Sarah Jane's tender heart every time she saw these wretched animals. She vowed to bring dry dog and cat food with her on her next trip to Egypt especially to bring to the Step Pyramid. On the way back to the hotel after the Step Pyramid the driver brought them to a rug factory where children worked on the intricate rugs. The driver told them that here the children received free schooling and were happy, but Sarah Jane felt sorry for these tykes and indeed for most of the young children in and around Cairo, many of whom seemed reduced to begging or selling cloth dolls from the tourists and seemed so pathetic it felt difficult to resist their entreaties.

Each night they went to the hotel's finest restaurant for dinner which featured International cuisine, and gave each woman a rose each evening as she entered and each diner a small box of candy as he or she left the restaurant. The food tasted so good, and the menu contained so many entrees that Sarah Jane and Robert continued to dine there each evening. The day after they visited the pyramids was the day that Robert was to fly alone to Luxor and Karnak. He planned to leave the hotel at 2:00 a.m. so as to make his 5:00 a.m. flight and have time to have breakfast in the hotel's restaurant which featured twenty-four hour service. When Robert left the hotel room Sarah Jane felt at sea and nervous despite the bravado she'd exhibited to Robert about her proposed day alone in Cairo. She kept hearing sounds as though someone were trying to open the door to her room. It was difficult failing back to sleep, but she finally drifted off for another hour or so, and then her adventurous day alone in Cairo begun. She ordered breakfast in her room, put on a robe and prepared to greet the room service waiter. Sarah Jane had discovered early on that the Egyptian men seemed to fancy American women, and they exhibited flirtatious tendencies which exceeded the bounds of propriety as far as she was concerned. She felt certain that the Egyptian men would never treat Egyptian women with the disrespect they constantly showed her. She'd experienced one incident of a guide at the Step Pyramid trying to pick her up, and one of the guides touched her improperly at the Cairo Museum while Robert looked elsewhere and then had the gall to ask Robert for baksheesh, which he gave not having witnessed the incident. So today while on her own she determined to be careful. After she tipped the room service waiter he seemed reluctant to leave, but as she didn't respond to his banter, he eventually departed. Sarah Jane faced the problem of having to travel to a hotel across the city to confirm travel arrangements, which would mean taking a taxi alone. Fortune shone on her as she left the hotel and headed toward the waiting taxi cabs as the same driver who had been chauffeuring them around Cairo and the environs hailed her from his waiting cab and announced himself willing to take her where she wanted to go and even to wait for her while she transacted her business.

With this knotty problem solved, Sarah Jane felt open to enjoy the experience of finding herself alone and on her own in Cairo. When her business about the travel arrangements concluded, Sarah Jane headed back with her friendly driver to her hotel where she explored the shops in the lobby and then went back to her room to order room service lunch. Brave as she felt, she didn't want to lunch alone in any of the hotel's fine restaurants. After lunch Sarah Jane ventured out alone and crossed the street in front of her hotel and headed for a shopping center which featured many elegant shops and the bookstore showing books written in English. She first entered a shop which featured beautiful Egyptian caftans where she tried on a gorgeous selection and finally bought a red Egyptian cotton one which had hand embroidery all around the collar and sleeves. Feeling exhilarated after her purchase of the authentic caftan, Sarah Jane visited the bookstore and purchased three or four novels to keep her amused for the rest of the afternoon and evening, as Robert wasn't expected back to the hotel until 10:00 p.m. Once back at the hotel the afternoon waned as she first watched an American movie on the television and then immersed herself into the novels managing to read two before dinner. This time when the room service waiter served dinner Sarah Jane found it harder than ever to get him to leave the room after she had tipped him. When he finally got discouraged and realized that she didn't desire his attentions he exited. Sarah Jane wondered if businesswomen on their own sometimes encouraged the amorous moves of some of these Egyptian men often enough to keep them trying.

After her solitary dinner Sarah Jane watched another American Movie on television and remembered that their driver had informed them that he learned English from watching television, She was grateful that the hotel's television offered this channel. As ten o'clock approached Sarah Jane felt expectant and too anxious to watch television, and she started reading the third novel. However, ten o'clock headed toward 11 o'clock, and still no sign of Robert. Sarah Jane began fretting as she knew that Robert had flown on a small Egyptian plane, and she feared an accident. By midnight she felt frantic, and when the phone rang she nearly jumped out of her skin. Leaping for the phone expecting to hear Robert's voice she became dismayed to hear a strange accented voice speaking in English.

"Yes, who is this?"

"It's the guide who arranged your husband's trip. His flight has been delayed, and he should he back to the hotel around 1:00 a.m."

"Well, that's a relief Thank you for calling."

At least she could put her fears to bed if not herself She was keyed up and still a bit fearful. Being alone in the hotel room at night spooked her. She eagerly looked forward to 1:00 a.m., but Robert didn't turn the key in the lock to the room until after 2:00 a.m. Sarah Jane greeted him with a kiss and much relief, and they spent a joyous hour talking about their separate adventures, and Sarah Jane felt proud to be able to relate her experiences alone in Cairo. Sarah Jane's Egyptian vacation had reached its climax with her day alone, and the rest of the week in Cairo passed pleasantly with fine dining experiences and many sight-seeing opportunities. By the end of the vacation, Sarah Jane felt like a seasoned traveler and found that she'd enjoyed the visit to Egypt almost as much as her dream trip to Paris. She now desired to travel as often as money and time allowed with Robert as her traveling companion.

The Raccoon Has Landed

Beth Ann's home resembled a wildlife sanctuary the last few years. Although Beth Ann's family didn't know why first a chipmunk took residence under the house in the front of the patio. and then birds made their nest each year in the Christmas wreath on the window if Beth Ann neglected to take the wreath down quickly after the holiday ended. The first time a nest appeared Beth Ann's husband, Jim, had been about to remove the wreath from the window when he shouted to Beth Ann,

"Quick. Come! You won't believe your eyes. There are robin's eggs inside a nest attached to this wreath. If I dare to budge the nest , the eggs will fall and break."

After running outside and checking the wreath, Beth Ann cried, "Oh, please leave the nest intact. We can't move it an inch until the baby birds are flying off on their own."

Jim agreed, and consequently they and their children watched as the robin sat on her eggs. They participated in

46

every stage of development from the hatching of the eggs to observing the mother and father robins fetch and feed worms and other matter to the babies. Beth Ann delighted when she observed the baby birds try their first flight with their new wings. Finally when the bird family took flight for the last time Beth Ann asked Jim to remove the wreath. In subsequent years they tried to take the wreath down before the birds could discover it, but the nesting situation took place at least once more over the next few years.

While the chipmunk and the birds posed little in the way of what could be termed a problem or even a nuisance, the next forest visitor posed a large problem when he and his pregnant wife paid a visit to their home. The new would be tenant and his wife, opossums, began building a nest in the attic actually carrying up branches for this purpose and getting in the attic somehow from the tall trees surrounding the house. Their residence in the attic bothered Beth Ann as she could hear them skittering overhead, but a very real problem cropped up when a disagreeable odor permeated the house, and Jim suspected that one member of the opossum family might have expired and its dead body might be causing the unpleasant smell. Jim and their oldest son, John, climbed up a ladder and entered the attic through the crawl space. John discovered the decomposing opossum offspring and removed it reluctantly, went as swiftly as possible back down the ladder and disposed of it. However, the incident bothered him tremendously as the offending odor seemed almost impossible to forget. However, after this the opossums mysteriously departed.

For some few months the neighborhood's wildlife seemed to ignore Beth Ann's house and yard Except, of course, for the three house cats who lived there as pets. Actually, Beth Ann frequently wondered why the wildlife bothered with their house since the possibly threatening cats lived there. One Spring before all these problems occurred a rabbit chose their backyard to make a nest for her baby rabbits. Beth Ann watched helplessly after the babies were born hoping that neither the cats nor any of her children or their friends would go near the fragile and unprotected nest. Beth Ann never discovered whether harm ever came to the baby rabbits and considered herself lucky not to know any upsetting details. After the opossum incident the next visitors to the attic were squirrels. They made Beth Ann so nervous that a wildlife organization came over at her request and trapped them. Unfortunately, they offered no helpful solutions as to how to stop this problem of unwanted forest creatures, and eventually Beth Ann's house became the residence of a family of raccoons. These creatures had everything they could desire here at their new home. Beth Ann and Jim caught them several times overturning their garbage cans and one night when they opened the back door and turned on the light, the fearless raccoons looked up from their ill-gotten feast of pizza and Chinese food which they were eating brazenly from the carton and stared at them. Beth Ann said,

"Are you having a good time for yourselves ? I see you're enjoying the food, and I assume that you enjoy the living arrangements as you don't seem to be wont to leave our hotel."

Each night while watching television in bed Beth Ann and Jim could hear the raccoons cavorting over their heads. To complicate the problem, rain had caused the bedroom roof to be weakened, and each time it rained the roof suffered more damage. Beth Ann became fearful that the raccoons would break through the weak spot on the ceiling and fall from the attic to the bedroom. One Halloween around midnight when the small ghosts and goblins had grabbed their candy bars and gone home and her own little witches and pirates lay sleeping and even Jim slept soundly next to her in bed Beth Ann turned on the television to watch "Rosemary's Baby", a long awaited treat for her As the horror unfolded on the screen the fearful sounds of the raccoons overhead seemed to increase in volume. Beth Ann's nerves became frayed with the combination of the terror produced by the movie and the frightening sounds of the animals overhead. As the movie reached its terrifying climax on the television and the mood music moved to a spooky crescendo, Beth Ann heard a deafening crash and watched in horror as a gigantic raccoon fell through the ceiling over the bed and landed on her leg before running off to the living room.

"Help," Beth Ann yelled, "the raccoon has landed. It's through the ceiling and running amok somewhere in the house."

Her shrieks woke the entire household. Jim leaped out of bed, and the children raced in to Beth Ann's bedroom from their own bedrooms.

"Where did you last see it heading'?" Jim asked.

"It ran toward the living room," Beth Ann answered.

The family entered the living room and Jim turned on the lights. There on top of the tallest bookcase in the room sat the raccoon staring at them out of huge frightened eves. Beth Ann figured that the raccoon must be as scared of them as they were of it. Jim went to the phone and called the police who answered by saying that they were on their way but that Jim should also call the animal warden. Jim swiftly compiled, and within minutes both the police and the animal warden arrived. However, everyone seemed to be at a loss as to know what to do. The animal warden seemed thrilled by the whole thing and demanded to see the hole in the bedroom ceiling saying,

"I wish I had a camera and some film."

The police offered no more in the way of helpful advice, and everyone stood gawking until Jim opened the front door and secured the door so it would remain open. The terrified raccoon upon realizing that an exit to the outdoors existed ran out. The immediate problem's being, solved, the police exited and the animal warden suggested that Beth Ann and Jim call a company called "Wildlife Unlimited" who he said would get rid of the raccoons and return them to the woods where they belonged. He then departed. Before Beth Ann and Jim could retire for the evening, Jim nailed a huge piece of wood over the hole in the ceiling so as to prevent the same thing from happening again that evening. The next day the wildlife people appeared with traps containing peanut butter to lure the raccoons, and within a couple of days the raccoon family had been trapped and taken to the woods.

It took Beth Ann's friend Lois' son Glen to find a final solution to the problem. He heard all about the incident from Lois and came over to see Beth Ann.

"You see," he said, "the problem is the tall trees all around your house front and back. That gives the animal friends their access to your attic. Trim the tall trees down, and your problem is solved. The wildlife will be unable to get in again. I can do this for you as I have a landscaping business as a sideline".

Beth Ann and Jim promptly hired Glen, and soon all the tall trees were trimmed to a safe level cutting off the wildlife's entrance to the attic. Beth Ann's house reverted back to a habitat for only humans and occasional house cats.

Kevin's Coming To Dinner

During the two years that Alice dated Kevin, she often accepted invitations from Kevin's family to come to dinner. Actually, Alice had partaken of Kevin's family's hospitality many times, and she felt comfort-able after a fashion in their company. However, until Alice and Kevin became engaged and Alice wore an engagement ring. Alice's family didn't reciprocate and extend Kevin an invitation to dinner. They seemed to feel that to do so constituted a formal acknowledgment on their part of their having accepted Kevin as a member of the family. Now that Alice had her ring, her mother finally invited Kevin over for a Sunday barbecue.

Alice knew that because of the formality surrounding this barbecue that Kevin felt as though he had to prepare to enter the arena and face down the lions. Fortunately, formal introductions could be ignored or tossed aside as Kevin knew the family well and had often engaged in discussions with Alice's mother and father and even her brother, Bill. Alice's family entered into the spirit of the occasion, and both of her parents out did themselves in the preparation of a feast. Alice's father barbecued a two-inch thick Sirloin steak and managed to see that it came off the grill medium rare as the family and Kevin liked it. Alice's mother prepared all the traditional accompaniments — fried onions, mushrooms, corn-on-the-cob, tossed salad, and as a special treat artichokes.

With a gorgeous meal like this one, and everyone's displaying good spirits, Alice thought that nothing could mar the day. However, when the bounteous feast reached the table Kevin put only steak, a bit of salad, and an artichoke on his plate while the rest of the group heaped their plates high. Alice realized that it must have been difficult for Kevin to try to eat normally with so many pairs of eyes watching his mouthfuls avidly trying to note something unusual.

Kevin had barely begun eating when Bill broke into howls of laughter, pointing at Kevin and saying,

"Look how he attacks the artichoke. He's cutting into it with his knife."

Unfortunately, Bill's laughter always set Alice off, and she burst into gales of laughter in spite of herself. Naturally, Kevin was confused as he had never seen nor heard of an artichoke before and he had tried to cut directly into it instead of prudently waiting to see what everyone else did with this strange vegetable. Kevin, looking bewildered found himself the object of hilarity. He seemed hurt and angry with Alice for joining Bill and her parents in the laughter. Alice expressed no surprise that Kevin never again attempted to try an artichoke, and she blamed herself for his aversion. Alice's father made a pronouncement that afternoon following dinner saying,

"Kevin has the appetite of a sparrow."

No matter what Kevin managed to eat at subsequent meals, and sometimes it consisted of a considerable amount, this description of his appetite stuck. Alice feared her mother got her feelings hurt because Kevin hadn't even sampled all the vegetables that she'd gone to such trouble to prepare. Later when they were alone, Alice questioned him about the vegetables as she couldn't quench her curiosity.

"I understand why you didn't attempt to finish the artichoke, but why did you reject my mother's excellent vegetables?"

"We were going out later, and I didn't want corn to get between my teeth or onions on my breath. As for mushrooms, I don't eat them."

Alice realized at this point that Kevin would never be a gourmet, but after all who cared what he did or didn't eat. Her main problem now seemed to be getting him to forgive her laughter at his expense.

"Kevin, Bill cracks me up. When he finds something funny I collapse into laughter. Please forgive me. Bill and I and even my parents behaved rudely."

At this stage in their romance Alice knew that there was little Kevin couldn't forgive in her, and that the rancor he felt would evaporate instantly. As always they sealed their making up with a kiss which Alice felt was all the sweeter because of what had gone before. After the kiss Kevin seemed to realize that his ordeal had come to an end. Never again would he be a complete novice at their dinner table. He couldn't have felt too insulted by Alice's father's statement about his appetite as he'd encountered the man's strong opinions on most subjects frequently in the past. Alice knew that he knew that her mother liked him which he demonstrated by asking Alice to explain why he'd rejected her variety of vegetables.

Alice realized that Kevin's invitation to dinner constituted a formal commitment to her parents even more than her engagement ring did. Now Alice knew plans for the wedding could commence. It seemed to Alice that Kevin had conquered the lions in their den and emerged victorious, albeit with aspersions cast upon his appetite.

Rome Alone

The Christmas season that year drifted by as smoothly as a new blanket of freshly fallen snow. As soon as Lily reached a sudden unexpected decision to gift her husband and son with trips to Italy for Christmas she found herself free to enjoy the festivities whirling around her. For the first time she heard the carols, looked at the lights and colorful decorations, and watched the shoppers exhausting themselves, and felt at peace with the season, and the meaning behind it. She'd never before experienced so much joy in concert with the season. She'd received a small legacy a few months before, so she could cope financially with a gift of such largesse. Her son had a month of freedom before he had to return to college, and her husband's firm gave him five weeks of vacation a year which he could carry over into the next year and he had fallen way behind in taking his vacations. Therefore, she could indulge her impulse and without telling, anyone she booked a vacation for three to Italy — a ten-day vacation featuring Rome, Venice, and Florence. Only when she knew the vacation plans had been firmed and confirmed, did she tell Larry, and Eric. Eric immediately asked,

"If Tom pays his own way can we book him too?"

"Sure," Lily answered. "You and Tom could learn a lot and enjoy the trip. You'll like it better with a pal. That way we could go on separate adventures."

Tom arranged for his trip with dispatch, and it worked out so that they could travel together on the same tour and the same flight to Rome. Lily informed her men that the trip to Italy comprised their entire Christmas present, and she proceeded to revel in the season's delights without the work or aggravation. Since the trip started on January 2nd, the usual New Year's depression got knocked out. Looking forward to the 2nd made Lily feel exhilarated rather than blue on New Year's Day and she even enjoyed taking the tree down for a change.

After a smooth flight during which Lily even slept a little, they arrived at the Rome airport. Rome at last. Their tour group leader found them instantly, and all followed easily. Their tour bus took them and the other members of their tour group to the Rome hotel. Once at the hotel and in the lobby waiting to go to their rooms, the tour guide told them all the features of the trip — the tours in each city, and the special attractions, and he told them they could pick and choose among them. Eric and Tom opted for almost all of the extras as did Larry, but Lily chose one day in Rome alone to get her hair done, wander about the city solo, and just catch her breath. So the final arrangement included a day in Rome alone for Lily while Larry and Eric went to Pompeii, and Tom opted to visit the Pope at one of his public appearances. The next day's tour of Rome which they all took included a visit to the Colosseum and a tour of the Sistine chapel. Fortunately, Lily discovered, many elevators helped them reach the Sistine Chapel, and the steps represented only a minor part of the trek. Once actually in the Sistine Chapel, Lily felt spellbound. The room which was bordered by benches attached to the wall had an empty space for her, and as soon as she sank onto it and gazed upward she felt awestruck. To actually see and contemplate Michelangelo's masterpiece seemed more than she could comprehend. The familiar figures of Adam, Eve and the angels loomed over her head. She felt lucky to be able to see this sight for herself, and she knew she'd etch the scene on her memory. Before returning to the hotel the tour stopped at St. Peter's, and Lily gazed at Michelangelo's Pieta. To visit Italy is to be put in awe of this artist who seems to summarize all that's beautiful in this country.

The next day started Lily's day in Rome alone. The morning's confusion gave the day a rocky start as Eric and Larry planned to go to Pompeii, but Eric felt too ill to go on a trip that started so early in the morning. Lily wondered if his reluctance harked back to the bottle of wine he'd finished almost single handedly the night before, but she held her tongue. Larry kissed Lily good-bye and wished her good luck on her day alone. Tom went off to see the Pope and left Eric in his room sleeping. Lily started off. The weather cooperated the entire time of their visit there — sunny and between 50 and 70 degrees. Lily noticed with a touch of amusement that the Italian women wore fur coats on a day when she wore a jacket and fell tempted to shed it after she'd walked a few blocks. She'd made her hair appointment the afternoon before using her hands to talk and pantomime washing and blow drying her hair and even received an estimated price. She arrived there without incident, and a little over an hour later with clean, shiny hair she hit the streets to wander Rome alone.

She found herself in a shopping area, a busy street with a beautiful park right across the way. No sooner had she begun window shopping when she noticed a man following her. Maybe his errand follows the same route as mine. She tried at first ignoring what seemed an intrusion on her privacy and/or person. Next she attempted darting into a store and staying for a while hoping, that she could lose him. No such luck. Each time she entered a store, there he lurked waiting for her exit. He kept grinning at her, and she began to wonder whether he had all his wits about him. He had average looks with an average height and weight, but the determined look in his eyes frightened her. She felt confused, but kept her senses and managed to hit upon a plan. She pretended to head into a store and when he moved to a vantage point to wait for her return she doubled back and went the opposite way. Before he realized her deception she found herself half a block in front of him. She moved swiftly until she could no longer see him, and she realized that her evasive tactics had worked. However, her glorious morning in Rome alone ground to a temporary halt, as she feared coming upon him again if she ventured again into the shopping district. Momentarily defeated and feeling breathless from fear and the narrow escape she headed for the hotel. Once there she discovered lunch being served in the hotel's restaurant, and she got a table and ordered lunch. She felt much better after a dish of pasta and salad and felt proud that she managed to pay the bill and leave a tip which seemed to please the waiter.

After lunch she sat in the hotel lobby and tried to rev her courage up to attempt another exploration of the city and the shopping area. She registered delight when she saw her son Eric come into the lobby from the street. He noticed her at once and came over to relate his adventures of the day.

"Hi, Mom. After I felt well enough to get up I telephoned to inquire whether I could still participate in the audience to see the Pope. I figured that since I missed Pompeii, I might as well attempt to see the Pope. The guide told me that tickets had already been issued, but I might luck into getting standing room or something."

"Did you get to see him?"

"I sure did. No one asked any questions I couldn't answer, and I just followed the crowd to where he planned to appear. What a thrill when he entered the room. It made me disappointed that I couldn't get closer or speak to him, but seeing him made it worthwhile."

After Lily told Eric about her misadventure of the morning, he suggested that the two of them go out together and explore some of Rome since Tom had joined a group from the tour after visiting the Pope and Larry remained absent on the trip to Pompeii. The two of them explored Rome to Lily's delight. She shopped and saw parts of the city the tour had thus far neglected. Rome though unlike Paris or London contained her own charm. Rome was Rome and could not be compared with any other city she'd seen before. When Larry returned from Pompeii full of excitement about what he'd experienced Lily told him about the man who'd accosted her. The rest of their dinner table made up of some of their fellow tour members overheard, and one young woman laughed and said,

"The same thing happened to me. The Italian men have no shame."

From Rome the tour took a bus to the outskirts of Florence. The guide stopped the bus on what he called the balcony — a scenic overlook square with a spectacular view of Florence. Florence contained a beauty that didn't disappoint Lily. She'd heard about Florence and its art treasures from her brother and found that the city lived up to her high expectations. When she and Larry stood in front of the David Lily felt as though the statute pulsated and wanted to leap off the pedestal. No reproduction she'd ever seen duplicated the beauty and power of the statue. She'd never appreciated the beauty of the human form in this depth before. The hotel in Florence had a dignity comprised of dark wood trim, parquet floors and Spanish or medieval tiles. Bells rang at 5 In the evening, and the sound of them filled Lily with peace. In Florence Lily and Larry toured the streets, visited the Duomo and stopped for gelato. On the way back to the hotel, Lily purchased a necklace from a store window which featured an array of necklaces containing miniature reproductions of old masters. The second day in Florence included a side trip to Pisa to see the leaning tower. The tower is a bell tower and really leans. Lily laughed aloud when she saw the tower, but unfortunately, her photographs taken that day failed to show just how much the tower leans. The tower and much else in Pisa is walled in. Pisa is the neighborhood of the author of Pinocchio and, therefore, many puppets could be purchased everywhere Lily looked. On the final evening in Florence the tour took a bus ride through the woods and into the country to a restaurant. The restaurant featured dancing, fine food and an Italian singer who crooned in Italian to some specially chosen women. Lily dreaded being chosen and felt too embarrassed to enjoy the song when the singer singled her out when he reached their table. On the way back From the restaurant the group sang songs led by the guide some of them in Italian.

Venice comprised the last city on their visit. It took a whole day to reach Venice from Florence, and for the trip to the hotel once they reached Venice they took a taxi boat. Boarding the taxi boat terrified Lily and only fear of her fellow travelers' derision enabled her to leap aboard. Venice took Lily's breath away. The boat taxi took them to the door of their hotel, they entered and unpacked. They began to walk with the group to dinner when they came on to St. Mark's Square unexpectedly. Lily experienced enchantment when she saw the square in the evening light. Nothing had quite prepared Lily for the beauty assaulting her senses. The next day St. Mark's Square looked equally lovely in the sunlight, and they stood and watched a model posing for a fashion picture with a myriad of pigeons alighting on her. In Venice the tour group visited a glass factory, and Lily made her major Italian purchase — a glass statue of a cat to add to her collection of cats. The statue may have been costly, but Lily felt the expense justified. Venice might have been hard to top, but it made up the last stop of the trip.

Lily survived Rome alone and fell in love with Italy. Visitors to Italy long to return in spite of the saying "See Rome and die." Lily firmly desired to see Rome again, and planned to make a return trip part of their future travel plans.

Susan And Betty
– A Friendship

How ironic that Toby represented the instrument that trumpeted the start of Susan's friendship with Betty. Sometime during the start of her eighth grade year Susan heard from one of her friends that her boyfriend of the minute happened to also like a girl named Betty. Since Betty had attended a different grade school, Susan had not known her prior to junior high. In fact, until her name came up in context with Toby's, Susan only knew her by sight.

Susan and Toby had started flirting In the spring of seventh grade, but they had not yet dated. First a movie double date had fizzled when the other girl couldn't make it. Then during the summer Toby had called Susan and invited her to spend an afternoon at his country club with him. The thought of appearing in front of a boy she hadn't yet dated in a swim suit had made Susan freeze with fear and had caused her to invent some excuse for not attending. Toby's best friend, Dennis, had reported to Susan that her refusal had really ticked Toby off'. According to Dennis, Toby had thought she'd been toying with him all along. Since now Susan's relationship with Toby could be described as limping along, she registered little surprise to hear this news about Betty.

Susan decided to meet her competition and perhaps take some action. Rather than hating Betty on sight, Susan liked her instantly. Betty exuded friendliness and seemed not to realize how beautiful she looked. As soon as Susan met Betty she realized why everyone liked her. After a few minutes of conversation Susan found that she and Betty shared a lot more in common than just Toby. Betty informed Susan that she had heard about her too, and for some reason she seemed to find the situation amusing. Just talking to Betty made Susan see how much humor this crisis could contain. Soon both she and Betty laughed, and Susan found that she'd been enjoying the whole encounter.

"Come over this afternoon after school and we'll decide what to do about Toby," Betty said.

During the long pleasant walk to Betty's house after school Susan found that the two of them never ran out of conversation. They exchanged histories and their likes and dislikes exclaiming each time they agreed. Susan discovered that they even had friends in common. Susan had heard that Betty's popularity included both boys and girls. She'd heard that Betty never stole her friend's boyfriends. Betty told Susan all about her large family which included two older brothers and several younger siblings. By the time they reached Betty's house Susan felt that they were already friends. Betty lived in a beautiful house, and her bedroom looked spectacular. It had a bed with a canopy—something Susan had only dreamed about.

Over cokes they discussed Toby. Susan told Betty about her relationship, brief as it had been with Toby. Betty said,

"I only met him a couple of weeks ago at dancing school where he danced with me once."

Susan and most of the junior high school kids attended a dancing school that held weekly dances. Susan said,

"I guess we can figure out what he thinks when we see who he dances with this Saturday night. I don't think he knows that we know about each other."

Now Susan felt that she and Betty shared a secret. They spent the next hour or so planning on how to keep a watch on him. On Saturday night Susan wore her prettiest gown to dancing class and waited to see what would happen with Toby. He came up to her immediately and they danced every dance together until about the middle of the evening. Midway during the dance he switched his attentions to Betty and danced for an equal amount of time with her. On Monday morning at school Susan ran into Betty in the halls and they laughed again.

"He gave us equal time," Susan said. "However, he gave you the last half. Which half do you think he considered more important?"

"I think it's a mute point, and we're back to zero information," Betty said.

Later that day Susan realized that Toby had heard about her friendship with Betty, and she communicated this knowledge to her. Betty said,

"Yes, he's heard, and I think he's puzzled. I even think it bothers him that we aren't upset with each other."

That afternoon in front of the school Toby and a friend of his came up to Susan and Betty as they stood talking . He bantered with both girls, and his friend, Dennis, joined in. Toby seemed bemused and Susan took a cue from Betty who seemed to be playing at being mysterious. Susan enjoyed watching Toby's confusion. After the boys left the girls talked about the situation again.

"Betty," Susan said. "I have decided that even if Toby chooses you it won't mar our friendship. I'm not sure he's worth it."

"I agree," Betty said. "We'll continue being friends no matter what happens."

The friendship did continue. Susan and Betty became close friends and remained friends throughout junior high and high school and beyond into their adulthood and marriages. Susan always found Betty's support there for her when she needed it. Susan remembered that Betty and Dennis had dated and that soon after the Toby incident she'd become involved with a boy named Jim, but she couldn't remember whom Toby had ended up with. Years later she asked Betty,

"Whom did Toby end up dating?"

"I don't know, but it sure wasn't one of us," Betty replied.

David Peacock

While perusing her high school yearbook Gabrielle came across her friend Jean's message that was sprawled across her pretty, pictured face. As she read the words always remember the fun we had together — the beach, slumber parties, and especially David Peacock — memories of David Peacock washed over her mind. Salty memories like the ocean, cool memories like the clubhouse pool on a hot day, and warm memories like bath water. She recalled how he had managed to shock all the groups at the core of the school when he moved to town. The son of the town's most pretentious bank's new President, David lived in the exclusive part of an exclusive town and arrived as the new kid at school wearing a black leather jacket as though in homage to James Dean or Marlon Brando. This in a town so preppie it represented one of the last to capitulate to rock and roll and worship at Elvis's heels. Gabrielle was one of the first girls in her crowd to place Elvis's picture on her wall, and for a while she stood alone.

Obviously, Gabrielle's group allowed, he must have come from a place where people besides hoods wore leather jackets. Here in Hillsboro where freshly creased khakis reigned, no one except juvenile delinquents would dream of making such a social gaff. Gabrielle soon learned that he did indeed come from Chicago so his mistake seemed understandable, but even after he'd been at the school long enough to notice that he stood alone, he never appeared anywhere without his jacket. He had silver blonde hair and blue eyes that penetrated, and he seemed to possess enough self-confidence to share. He showed no neediness concerning making friends. In fact, although he was friendly, he acted like he didn't care whether people flocked to his side or not. Of course, this attribute drew first the boys and then, showing relief, the girls who had always seemed to think him a hunk.

At the first high school dance after his acceptance, David demonstrated a talent that most of the other boys in Gabrielle's crowd lacked — he could dance. Soon, Gabrielle realized, every girl in the high school longed to be his partner at the dances or, wonderful thought, to actually go to a dance with him. Fortunately for the girls, David seemed to be a field player, taking a different girl to each dance. Gabrielle lucked out by being his date to a dance that featured a dance contest. The judges chose a Lindy as the particular number for the contest. All the couples who desired to enter the contest were to begin dancing until tapped on the boy's shoulder, and then they were to leave the dance floor. Gabrielle trusted David's expertise as a dancer and followed his lead expecting at any moment to be yanked from the floor. She felt exhilarated as well as sweaty and she felt her long black hair flying and hitting her in the eyes, but she danced on. Soon the couples remaining on the floor were down to ten, then five, and finally two — she and David and the most popular couple in the school, A dance never seemed as long as this one, and just as she felt she might topple over from nerves and exhaustion she realized that she and David danced alone on the floor. She knew that she'd never forget the cheers that greeted their triumph, and they each won a trophy — the first prize that Gabrielle had ever won.

After winning the dance contest, Gabrielle thought she might be falling for David. She knew this posed a problem because of David's propensity to date a different girl each time he went out on a date. She told herself that she had as much chance of landing David as she did of landing Elvis himself She took great care not to mention her feelings to anyone not even Jean, her best friend at that time. Fortunately, Gabrielle found herself at this point in her high school life with several boys asking her out. This proved to be a distraction, but she still fantasized in secret about David. Fortunately, David had chosen to join Gabrielle's crowd. He often showed up when the group was just hanging out and seemed to be always present when the crowd took a picnic to the beach or went as a group to an amusement park. Each time he arrived with another attractive girl on his arm, Gabrielle's jealousy burned. She tried not to show it as green didn't become her. As bad as she felt about his popularity with her friends, at least he'd not as yet chosen one special girl. As long as this remained true, Gabrielle nurtured her crush and refused to allow hope to die completely. She spent time puzzling aloud with her friends as to why he refused to commit to anyone even for a short time.

Jean said, "Maybe he really hasn't found any one of us pretty or popular enough."

"That's ridiculous," Gabrielle replied. "He seems to really appreciate each one of us. When he kissed me goodnight after the dance he acted like he enjoyed it and seemed reluctant to stop."

Unfortunately, Gabrielle discovered the answer to the mystery of David's lack of commitment too soon after this conversation. David, himself, told her.

"Gabrielle I want you to know this first. My father took a better job, and we're moving again. It seems like every time I get to care about a town and discover friends we move again. Had that not been true, I certainly would have taken you out more than once. But, Gabby, we still have the dance contest win to remember. Don't we?"

Gabrielle tried to express to David how much that date had meant to her. Strangely, she never mentioned her feelings for David to anyone else even after this conversation. David's stay in Hillsboro may have been a short one, but he remained in the hearts of everyone who'd known him as Jean's words in the yearbook stated. When Gabrielle looked at Jean's smiling face and reread the words written over it she said aloud,

"Yes, Jean, I remember David Peacock."

About The Author

Susan C. Barto was *born* on the beautiful day of June 21, 1941. The beloved child of Eda and Wiliam Forcellon. As she grew up she met a terrific man (Harry W. Barto) who later became her loving husband. Later Susan gave birth to a handsome baby boy (William M. Barto).

Susan's *educational* background was developed at Katherine Gibbs School and Union College, NJ. She has traveled extensively to Egypt, Italy, England and France.

She has experience with two years Legal Secretary - Legislative Aide; A writer for the last ten years. Her *memberships* include President Friends of the Hunterdon Museum of Art — New Providence Library Board, NJ — Raritan Valley College Book Group.

Susan Barto's *honors* are: Golden Certificate Award, Drury's Publishing™ — Plaque from Library Board, Listed in 1999-2000 Who's Who In The East and 2000 Who's Who In America, and Who's Who In Literary Achievement.

Her *publishing credits* include eleven stories published

with Creative With Words, One story published with Yesterday's Magazette, One story published with Writer's Guidelines and News, One story published with Good Old Days, and several stories published with Drury's Publishing™, along with four books of stories published by Drury's Publishing™.

On a more *personal note* Susan C. Barto says: ***"I love to write. Writing defines who I am."***